Woodland Magic

FOX CUB RESCUE

FOX CUB RESCUE

JULIE SYKES
illustrated by KATY RIDDELL

Piccadilly
PRESS

First published in Great Britain in 2022 by
PICCADILLY PRESS
4th Floor, Victoria House, Bloomsbury Square, London WC1B 4DA
Owned by Bonnier Books
Sveavägen 56, Stockholm, Sweden
www.piccadillypress.co.uk

A CIP catalogue record for this book is available from the British Library.

ISBN: 978-1-800-78142-9
Also available as an ebook and in audio

1

Typeset by DataConnection Ltd
Additional design by Perfect Bound Ltd
Printed and bound in Great Britain by Clays Ltd, Elcograf S.p.A.

Piccadilly Press is an imprint of Bonnier Books UK
www.bonnierbooks.co.uk

For Polly Nolan with love and a sprinkle of Woodland Magic

Chapter One

'Sorry, Nutmeg, but you have to stay here today,' Cora told the little brown mouse perched on the windowsill of her tree-house home. 'I'm not going to school. I'm old enough to go rewilding now in the Big Outside!'

Cora showed Nutmeg her new woodland bag, made from spiders' thread. It wasn't sticky and it didn't cling to her hands like an actual web. It was soft and silky and incredibly strong. The bag had two straps so that it could be worn as a backpack. It was infused with magic to make it stretch so that anything could be squashed inside – even an elephant if you ever needed to move one. The bag had several compartments to keep stuff safe. The only things inside it now were Cora's work tools: a spade, a rake and a garden fork.

Nutmeg's whiskers twitched as she sniffed at the bag. Cora pulled it away,

worried that the little mouse would nibble a hole in it. Just then, Jax ran up the spiral stairs that wrapped around the tree's outer trunk. His pounding feet made all the branches tremble. Nutmeg scampered out of the window and along the branch, her long tail disappearing into the spring leaves.

Cora went to open the top door.

'Ready?' said Jax.

'I've been ready for ages.'

'No school today,' said Jax with a wide smile.

Cora grinned back at him. 'No school for ever if we pass the trial. I hope we don't stay trainees for long. I can't wait to be a fully trained Keeper.'

Cora's stomach hopped like it was full of baby frogs. She wanted to get started. It was just a shame that Nutmeg couldn't come too, like she had sometimes when Cora went to school, but Cora was scared that Nutmeg might get lost in the Big Outside.

'No more boring lessons with Signor Dragonfly. Keepers get to go rewilding on their own,' said Jax.

There were Keepers all around the world. The ones living in the Hidden Middle of the Whispering Woods had been there since the Stone Age. Keepers cared for the countryside, rewilding it by doing things that helped nature to recover when the Ruffins were careless with it. Some of the rewilding tasks were small, like sowing seeds, and others were much bigger, like planting a whole forest to help prevent a flood.

'I hope we don't see any Ruffins,' said Cora.

Keepers went to work very early in the morning and some of the adults went last

thing at night, when most Ruffins were
tidied away in their houses. The rest of the
time they spent in the Hidden Middle,
chilling, sleeping or doing chores.

Ruffins were scary. They were so big,
like giants – even the young ones. Cora
had almost been flattened by a Ruffin
child once. Keepers were usually very good
at staying out of sight but Cora had got
distracted and hadn't seen him when he
came running at her through the ferns.

Luckily his
funny rounded
ears didn't seem
to work as well
as her pointed
ones and he
didn't hear Cora
scream. She had
been forced to

use her long fingers to shower his feet with a
magic mist so that he skimmed over her! He
ran off, unaware that he could have stamped
on her or taken her home to eat. That was the
Keepers' woodland magic for you. It wasn't
the big zappy kind that could make a Ruffin
fly or turn him into a stinky badger's bottom,
but it was very useful all the same.

Cora shouldered her bag. 'I wonder what
we'll be doing today.'

Not only did the Keepers care for the
countryside but they lived off it. Every day,
at times when most Ruffins were still in bed,
Keepers went into the Big Outside to gather
nuts, seeds, fruit, wood, fur and anything else
from nature's larder that might be useful.

It was up to Scarlet Busybee to give each
Keeper a task. Scarlet was also in charge of
the stores where everything they collected
was kept, and the workshops where a team

of Keepers turned it into something useful.
'*From nature's floor to our door, caring for the
countryside and taking only what we need!*' as
Scarlet was fond of telling everyone.

'We'll soon find out. Race you to the
Bramble Door!' Instead of using the spiral
steps, this time Jax put his leg over the
handrail and slid down it, his blue hair
streaming behind him.

'Bye, Mum,' yelled Cora, as she followed him, also using the handrail as a slide.

'Stay safe, keep out of sight and don't get caught by the Ruffins,' her mother's voice floated after her. Mum didn't go rewilding much these days. She worked in the popular Keepers' cafe, the Crow's Nest.

Cora and Jax ran through the forest to the thick bramble hedge surrounding the village. There was only one door and they queued to go through it behind their friends, Trix and Nis. Nis was munching on a toasted fern dipped in honey.

'Yum,' said Cora. 'That smells lovely, Nis. Is it another of your creations?'

Nis took after his dad: they had the same shade of red hair and they both loved cooking. Nis was always coming up with delicious twists on foods. 'Elderflower and jasmine honey,' he agreed with a nod.

Trix had purple hair that she wore in a bun skewered with a small screwdriver. Trix was into science and engineering and never went anywhere without a few of her tools.

Cora crossed her eyes and stuck her tongue out at Jax as her arch enemy, Penelope Lightpaw (or Perfect Penelope as Cora secretly called her), joined the queue.

Penelope tucked a strand of pink hair behind her ear as she looked Cora up and down. She made a face like she was drinking a sour-berry smoothie. 'Were you late getting up or is something nesting in your hair? Winnie, lend her a brush.'

Penelope's friend Winnie scowled. 'Eew! No!'

'Ew!' Cora agreed. She ruffled her long green hair with her hands, deliberately

making the tangles worse, and turned her
back on Penelope and Winnie.

As they shuffled forward in the queue,
Cora wished Nis would hurry up and
finish his fern before she started dribbling.
Her own breakfast of boring old acorn
pancakes had been ages ago. But at last
Nis and Trix stepped up to the Bramble
Door. Cora's tummy tightened. It was
their turn!

Scarlet Busybee tapped her pencil to her
mouth. She looked from her list to Cora and

Jax. 'Hmmm,' she said.
'Is it wise to let you two
go rewilding together?'
Cora stood up straighter
and gave Scarlet a trustworthy
smile. It wasn't Cora's fault
that she often got into

scrapes with Jax. Mischief seemed to follow them around.

'You can look as innocent as you like,' said Scarlet, 'but Jax and you have a nose for trouble.'

Cora glanced at Jax. He widened his eyes back at her then quickly looked away. His shoulders heaved as he tried not to laugh. Cora guessed he was remembering the unfortunate incident with the feathers in their hopefully *last-ever* science lesson. Cora swallowed back a snort.

'The new play park next door to the football pitch,' said Scarlet, finally making up her mind to trust them. 'The Ruffins bulldozed a field of wildflowers when they built it.' She handed them each a bag of flower seeds. 'Go and reseed the land around the park. Don't let me down, you two. Remember, you have to return by dawn and you are on trial. I can send you back to school at any time.'

Cora had no intention of going back to school, not ever. 'We'll reseed what's left of the field and we'll also fill our woodland bags with lots of brilliant stuff for the store,' she promised.

'Hmmm, we'll see,' said Scarlet. 'Empty eggshells are on my Want List. I need two, big enough to make headlights for Grandmother Sky's new car. I shall fill the shells with starlight-powered glowing flower petals. I also need pine cones, as many as you can find. We need them for the little ones in the kindergarten to make dye-dipped pine-cone bunting to hang around the palace and the whole of the Hidden Middle. These are urgent Wants. The car and the bunting must be ready in time for Grandmother Sky's annual birthday regatta in a few weeks. It's going to be the best one ever this year.'

'Eggshells and pine cones,' said Cora, edging towards the door.

Scarlet held up a hand to stop her. 'Wait, please, for the Warning: *Stay out of sight and don't get caught by the Ruffins.*'

And with the Want and the Warning delivered, Scarlet finally stood aside.

Stepping through the Bramble Door with Jax, Cora fell silent. This was a special moment. It was their first time on their own in the Big Outside.

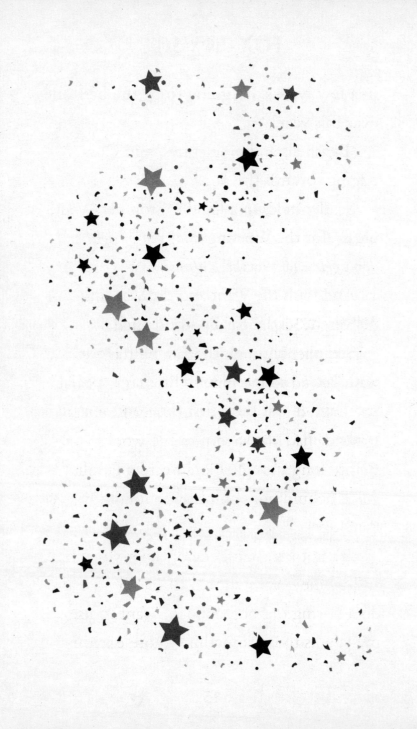

Chapter Two

The Whispering Woods seemed suddenly much larger now that Cora was allowed to be there without a grown-up. She looked past Jax for the other Keepers but they had vanished into the woods. Before long though, Cora heard a familiar voice behind her complaining loudly. Perfect Penelope!

'It's not fair,' said Penelope, her voice high and whiney. 'Why should I have to go and do a boring old bug count? I want to use my talents to do something more exciting.'

Cora didn't want to listen to Penelope telling everyone how clever and perfect she was. She'd had enough of that at school. 'Let's go this way,' she said to Jax, peeling off onto a different track.

As Penelope's voice faded Cora breathed in deeply. The fresh air filled her lungs, making her head feel floaty. The Whispering Woods were dark and mysterious. In the half-light between night and day, Cora could only just make out the shapes of the trees, roots and bushes around her.

'A wood-pigeon feather!' Cora's eyes lit up as she swooped on the black, white and grey striped feather. Scarlet needn't have worried. Cora had this!

'Great find!' said Jax, sounding envious.

Cora grinned as she removed her woodland bag from her back. It felt good to be the first one to find something useful.

'Wait! Don't put it away yet, give it here.' Jax held out his hand for the feather.

'What are you going to do with it?' Cora held on to it tightly.

'Give it here and I'll show you.'

Cora didn't want to let the feather out of her sight. It was the first thing she'd collected, but that sounded silly. She passed it over while fighting back the urge to tell him to be careful with it.

Jax grinned.
Holding the
feather by its
quill he tickled
Cora with it.

'Stop,' she
giggled. 'Jax,
don't! You'll
break it.'

'Do you surrender?'

'Yes!' Gasping for breath, Cora fell on the ground clutching her tummy. Her foot sank into a pile of leaves, uncovering a shrivelled beech nut left over from the autumn.

Jax swooped on the nut. 'Older than Grandmother Sky,' he said, holding it up.

'Nothing is older than Grandmother Sky,' said Cora.

Grandmother Sky was the Queen of the Hidden Middle. She was very grand and ancient and kept her age a secret. Not even the prince and princess knew exactly how old she was.

Jax put the beech nut into his woodland bag and gave Cora back her feather. She put it in her bag, making sure it went into an empty compartment and not the one that held her work tools.

'It's a good start,' Cora said as they went on their way.

As they approached the edge of the woods, Jax said, 'Look, we've caught up with Trix and Nis. What are they doing?'

'Have you lost something?' Cora asked as they came up behind them.

'I've found a patch of self-heal,' said Trix pointing to a thick clump of purple flowers. 'I'm taking a few for the store.'

'Good find,' said Cora. Self-heal was always in demand as one of its uses was to make a balm for wounds.

'We'd best get going,' said Trix. 'Scarlet's sent us to a house on the edge of the Ruffin village that's just had an extension. Several trees were cut down to make space for it and we're going to plant some new ones at the bottom of the garden. Then after that, we're going to the allotments.

Scarlet said it's a great place for finding forgotten vegetables.'

'It is.' Nis nodded. 'That mixed bake we had yesterday at the Crow's Nest, the parsnips came from a compost heap there.'

'Yum,' said Trix. The Crow's Nest, run by Nis's dad, was a two-storey tree-house cafe with a viewing platform, a rope bridge, a fun twisty chute and a staircase. The cafe was at the top of the tallest oak in the Whispering Woods. It was a popular meeting place and all the Keepers loved hanging out there. 'Your dad's an ace cook, Nis. I hope we find something tasty for him.'

They parted, Trix and Nis one way, Cora and Jax another. Cora walked with her eyes on the ground, hoping to find an empty shell that a chick had hatched from, or some pine cones. Unlikely, she knew. It wasn't

often you found an eggshell, and there
were hardly any fallen cones left now. The
Keepers had already collected most of them
and would have to wait for the autumn for
more to come down from the trees.

Cora and Jax left the woods and were
approaching the stone bridge that arched
over the river at the edge of the trees
when something rushed past them. Caught
in the whoosh of air, Cora almost fell over.
She pushed her hair out of her eyes.

'Fox cubs!' she breathed.

The cubs were taller than Cora. She
motioned to Jax to follow her to the foot
of a tree where they could crouch, safely
out of the way behind a barrier of gnarled
roots. The cubs ran in circles, chasing,
leaping and tumbling, their bushy tails
streaming behind them like red and gold
flames.

'Cora!' Jax's warm breath suddenly tickled her ear. 'We should go before the Big Outside gets cluttered up with Ruffins.'

'In a pip!' Cora wanted to stay and watch the cubs. 'Shhh,' she added as Jax, who hated sitting still, began to fidget.

A bark came from the forest. The fox cubs stopped playing to listen. Another bark, closer now, and the cubs replied with high-pitched yaps. A mother fox loped out of the trees and the cubs crowded round her, nuzzling at her with their noses. She nuzzled them back, and then they left together, vanishing into the woods.

Cora sighed happily. 'Weren't they just the cutest? Now we can go!'

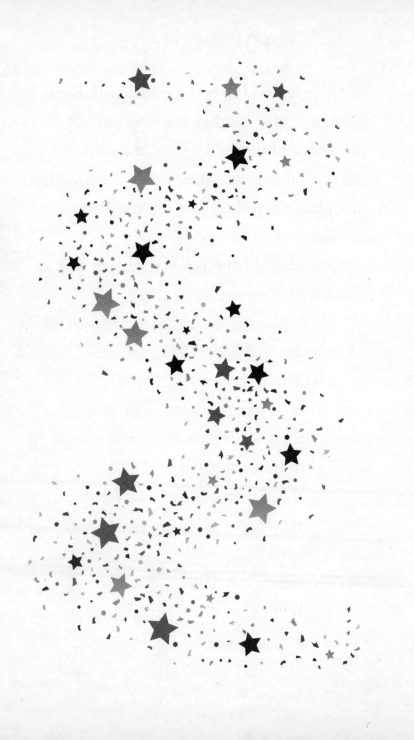

Chapter Three

They crossed the river, running over the bridge quickly because there was nowhere to hide from a Ruffin if one came along. Cora threw an anxious look at the sky. It felt lighter out here in the open without the cover of the trees.

Soon the sun would rise. The Ruffins would tumble from their beds and then they'd be everywhere, filling the Big Outside with noise, leaving their rubbish strewn about and generally making a mess.

Cora and Jax hurried past the boatyard and its cafe. They left the main track and ran across the football field to the play park. Cora gasped. She remembered when the play park had been a meadow. She'd passed through it several times when they'd been out on school trips with Signor Dragonfly. The long grass that had once rustled and chirped with insects had all gone. So had the wildflowers that had brightened the green with rainbows of colour. Now the earth was smothered with a boring grey surface. The play park was enclosed by hard metal railings and the strip of land around the outside was empty and bare.

Cora peered through the railings at the play equipment. 'It's huge!' she breathed. 'The slide is as big as a mountain!' The gap between each step on the ladder was almost as tall as her.

Jax ran to the gate. 'Let's try it out.'

'We're supposed to be planting seeds.'

'Just one go. Pleeeeasy squeezy! I've never seen a slide this steep and it's made from metal. I bet it goes really fast. There's plenty of time to have one teensy go before we start rewilding.'

Cora was torn. She hated to see the earth so empty and sad, but Jax loved fast things. Since he'd stopped to let her watch the fox cubs it was only fair that she went on the slide with him.

Jax sensed her hesitation and made huge eyes at her just like Nutmeg did when she wanted a treat. Cora's resolve not to get distracted collapsed. The gigantic slide looked so much fun. One pip of a go wouldn't hurt. There'd still be plenty of time to sow their seeds.

'All right then.'

The gate had been made to let Ruffins
in and out but clearly not a tiny Keeper
who didn't even come up to a Ruffin child's
knees! The gate had a snippy spring that was
impossible for Cora or Jax to open. They
pushed together, leaning their backs against
it, but each time the gate shifted the snippy
spring snatched it closed again. The railings
weren't wide enough to walk through but
by turning sideways and breathing in Cora
and Jax managed to squeeze between them.

'Phew!' Jax held
his tummy. 'It's a
good thing that
I didn't have an
extra helping of
daffodil porridge
this morning.'

'Race you to the slide!' said Cora, taking off at a sprint.

'I won!' said Jax, overtaking her and reaching it first.

The steps of the slide were so far apart that Cora wished she had a rope to help her to climb them. She was red-faced and breathing hard when she finally reached the top. She sat down next to Jax, with her legs resting on the slide's shiny chute.

'Look, Jax, there's the Ruffin village. It's so tiny from up here.'

'It's weird! The houses aren't hidden away like ours. Anyone can see them.'

Cora swivelled round to look back at the Whispering Wood. It was impossible to see into the Hidden Middle where she lived, but even if she had been able to, she wouldn't have seen her house or even her village. Keepers' tree houses, with their fantastic

turrets, towers, chimneys and twisty steps, blended perfectly with their surroundings.

'Ruffin houses are on show because they don't need to hide from us or anyone.'

'Why should we hide from them? It's our world too,' said Jax indignantly.

'Jax, you know why! Remember the book!'

Almost a hundred years ago, a Keeper had found a book called *Nursery Rhymes* – rules written in verse for Ruffin children. The book had been dropped in a puddle and most of it was too damaged to read but it was clear from the few surviving pages that Ruffins weren't friendly. On one page there was a rhyme about telling tales. If you were a tell-tale nit, so the rhyme went, then the Ruffins would cut out your tongue and feed it to their puppy dogs. On another page a small Ruffin was shoving a

 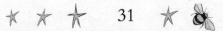

cat called Pussy down a well. But the worst
rhyme of all, the one that terrified Keepers
the most, was about an unfortunate Keeper
that their ancestors had nicknamed Jack.
A lot of the print was smeared but it was
easy enough to guess how the rhyme went.
Since finding the book, every Keeper
was taught that rhyme as soon as they
could talk.

'*Fee fi fo fum, I smell the blood of Jack
Keeper. YUM!*' Cora whispered.

'I guess.' Jax sighed, cutting her off before
she recited the whole thing. 'But I'd still love
to see inside one of their houses. Imagine all
the stuff they must have.'

Cora sniffed. 'Too much stuff. It's why
they're so careless with the countryside.'

'They think that if they use it up, they
can replace it,' Jax agreed. 'Come on, let's try
this slide out.'

Cora looked down the chute. It was so steep! It made her tummy wobble like frog spawn.

'Um . . .'

'See you at the bottom!'

There was a rush of air and the space beside Cora was suddenly empty.

Jax was a blur as he slid away from her. Seconds later she heard his faint cry of 'Cattywumps!'

Cora peered down the chute. Jax waved up at her. She sat very still while she decided how to get back to the ground. She could use the chute or the ladder. *Neither*, she thought with a shudder, but she couldn't stay here all day. Taking a deep breath, she closed her eyes and pushed off. Cold air rushed at her face, pinching her cheeks. Her eyes streamed and her hair flew out in long green ribbons. She opened her eyes and

saw the ground rush up to meet her as she
flew from the end of the chute. She landed
with a crunch and a hop, her arms whirling
as she tried to keep her balance. Her heart
pounded against her chest but she couldn't
stop grinning.

'Let's go again!'

'One go only, that's what we agreed,' said
Jax with a straight face.

'Jax!' wailed Cora. 'I've got to have
another go . . .' She stopped. He was teasing
her. 'Fluff head,' she said, bumping him with
her shoulder.

Jax bumped her back. 'Race you to the top!'

The slide was so much fun that one more
turn turned into two and then three. Then
Jax suggested that they race each other,
sliding down together.

'Rematch!' wailed Cora when he beat
her.

The slide racing turned into a competition that Cora and Jax were both determined to win. The score was twenty each when they sat at the top of the slide for a final decider race.

'Hi, lo, GO!' Jax yelled and he pushed off.

Cora went so fast she could hardly catch her breath but Jax was even faster, beating her to the ground by a spider's thread. He landed on his bottom by the swings.

Cora roared with laughter.

'What's that?'
Dusting the grit
from his woven
grass jeans, Jax
ran under a
swing seat. 'It's a
broken eggshell,'
he whooped.
Jax couldn't stop

grinning. The shell was a creamy brown with jagged edges. He held it up to his eyes and peered at it. 'It's from a wood pigeon. I know what you're thinking – it's not very pretty, but it's big enough to fill with petals.'

'I'm thinking it's brilliant!' said Cora, loyally.

Cora could imagine Scarlet's face when she went through Jax's woodland bag and found the piece of shell. *I knew I was right to trust you to work with Cora,* she would say. *This is exactly what I need to make one headlight.* Scarlet would then tell Grandmother Sky – she always asked who had found the best stuff on her daily workshop visit. Grandmother Sky would write the Keeper's name in her book and four times a year she held a party to reward those best Keepers. It was Cora's dream to get invited to a palace party.

Grandmother Sky was desperate for
Scarlet to finish her car, which would run
on a special mixture of forest berry juices
and Keepers' woodland magic. Grandmother
Sky was finding it hard to get around these
days especially in the Big Outside. It made
her sad because she loved travelling almost as
much as she loved parties. With her annual
birthday regatta coming up, Grandmother
Sky wanted the car ready for her special
moonlight party at the river.

'We'd better get on and plant our seeds.
Who knows, we might even find the other
piece of the egg.' Jax's words were drowned
out by the low bellow of a horn. His eyes
widened in horror. 'That can't be Tyr
already?'

The horn sounded again. Cora stared
back at Jax in disbelief. 'It is!'

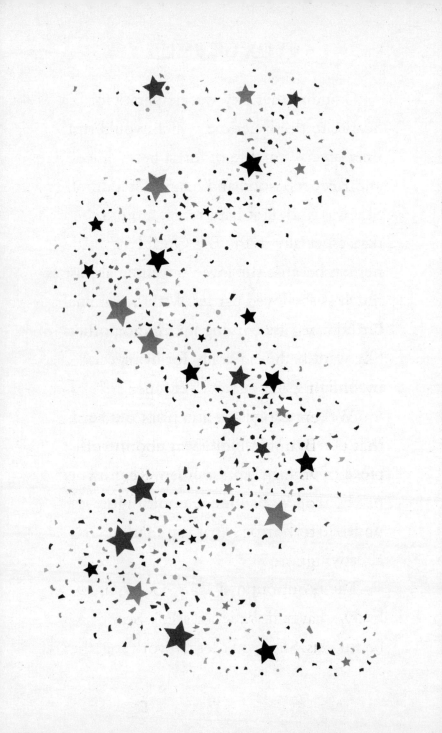

Chapter Four

Tyr was an ancient Viking horn that
had been made hundreds of years ago
by one of Cora and Jax's Keeper ancestors.
Since then, it had been used as a warning
that the Bramble Door was about to be
closed. On hearing the horn, Keepers
had to stop what they were doing
immediately and return home. Keepers
did not ignore Tyr.

'We're out of time,' Jax gasped.

'We haven't sown our seeds. Scarlet will
be furious. She won't let us work together

again. She might even send us back to school!' said Cora.

'But we've got a wood-pigeon shell. It was on the Want List, and there's the feather and the nut.'

'Will it be enough?' said Cora. Scarlet was very strict. The best stuff counted for nothing if she thought you hadn't worked hard.

Jax glanced around. There was something at the far end of the play park.

'What's that over there by that pile of rubbish near the shelter? It might be another shell.'

Cora panicked. If they found Ruffin rubbish, they were supposed to tidy it into a Ruffin bin. 'Jax, stop! There isn't time to go and look.'

Across the
football field
a stream of
Keepers were
hurrying back to
the Whispering
Woods.

'Jumping
jackdaws! Why
did we spend so
long on the slide?'

Jax shrugged as if he wasn't bothered but
Cora knew different. Jax wasn't all about
going fast and having fun. He was just as keen
to become a fully trained Keeper as she was.
It was all they had ever talked about at school.
Cora looked around her. The sun was rising
up from below the horizon in a blaze of gold.

'We really should go,' she said.

'But what if that *is* the other bit of the egg?'

Cora hesitated. Two pieces of shell, especially if they were matching, would be an excellent find and might be enough to keep Scarlet happy since she needed them for car headlights. But once the Bramble Door was shut, it wouldn't be opened again until sunset. Tough luck if you were left outside in the daylight with the Ruffins at large. The Hidden Middle of the Whispering Woods had to be kept a secret for the safety of all Keepers living there. It would be terrifying and dangerous to be stuck in the Big Outside in daylight. 'There really isn't time, Jax.'

Jax nodded. Cradling the shell in his hand he headed for the railings.

'Show-off!' muttered Cora. The shell would be protected by woodland magic if he put it inside his woodland bag, but Jax wanted everyone to see what he'd found!

Cora felt bad about not completing their task but there'd be trouble of a worse kind, both with Scarlet and their parents, if they didn't make it home! She squeezed through the play-park railings after Jax and ran across the football field. It seemed twice as big as it had done earlier, and very open with nowhere to hide. Steam was pouring from a vent in the back of the cafe. A metal shutter rattled as the boathouse opened. Seconds later a Ruffin came from round the side of the building. Cora's heart sped up but luckily the Ruffin was in a hurry and didn't notice her or Jax.

They ran on, crossing over the

bridge and entering the Whispering Woods.
Cora wanted to stop for a rest – her heart
was hammering faster than a woodpecker
tapping a tree. The Horn of Tyr sounded
again. Five short blasts – the final call. The
Bramble Door was about to close.

'Run!' hollered Jax.

'Running!' puffed Cora. Her lungs
burned and her arms pumped. They
weren't going to make it. Pictures of her
and Jax hiding in the trees while Ruffins
hunted for them flashed through Cora's
head.

'I'm using woodland magic!' she gasped
out. Pointing at her toes, Cora blasted them
with magical mist. Jax did the same and
they sped up, reaching the Bramble Door
on superfast feet just as it shut. They hurled
themselves at the closing gap, forcing their
way through and almost getting crushed.

There was a crunch as they landed in a heap of tangled limbs.

'What is the meaning of this?' Scarlet's eyes blazed as she stared down at Cora and Jax.

'Sorry! We . . .' Cora was struggling for breath. She wished she had a good excuse for arriving back so late.

Jax let out a wail. 'Cattywumps! I crushed the shell. I landed on it when I fell.' In his hand, the bird's egg was smashed into tiny pieces.

Scarlet inhaled slowly. 'Stop waving that around. Give it here.' Her eyes glittered with anger as she examined the fragments. 'Inexcusable. Go and wait for me in the stores. Now. Before I throw you back to the Big Outside with the Ruffins. It's no less than you deserve for spoiling such a valuable piece of nature.'

Cora was hot from running and even hotter with shame as she and Jax made their way through the trees to the square at the centre of the Hidden Middle where the school, the stores and Grandmother Sky's palace were located.

'Did you see Scarlet's face? I thought she was going to explode,' Jax whispered.

Cora glanced over her shoulder. Scarlet's hearing was even sharper than Signor Dragonfly's, but she must have taken another path as she wasn't behind them.

'She'll fix it,' said Cora sounding more confident than she felt. 'Scarlet's good at mending stuff. She'll glue it back together.'

'I hope she can. She might even be able to mend it with woodland magic. It would be so cool if Scarlet could use my wood-pigeon shell in Grandmother Sky's car.'

'Very cool.' Cora's tummy knotted with worry. Unlike Jax she wasn't convinced that collecting a feather and a wrinkled nut was enough for one outing. She hoped she was wrong. She didn't want to be sent back to school after just one mission.

There was a long queue at the stores and it trailed outside. Cora and Jax took their place at the end. Further along the line Nis and Trix waved at them in relief.

'You made it back!' said Trix.

'You had us worried,' Nis added.

The queue slowly moved forward and at last Cora and Jax could enter the stores. Haru Saltysea, Scarlet's assistant, was emptying the woodland bags on to a long wooden counter. Next to him, Scarlet examined everything, then sorted it into the crates behind her on the ground.

Later on, Scarlet and her helpers would put the things in the correct place in the stores.

Penelope and Winnie were just ahead of Cora and she could hear them arguing in fierce whispers.

'The pine cone was mine,' hissed Winnie. 'I climbed up to get it.'

'But I saw it first.' Penelope clutched her woodland bag as if Winnie might try to snatch it away.

Cora's attention wandered as she waited for her turn. She loved the stores. Once it had been a badgers' sett but the badger family had moved on, leaving behind a maze of underground chambers linked by tunnels. It had been Grandmother Sky's idea to turn it into the nature store. Over the years the stores had been extended several times to make room for the ever-growing quantity of things collected from the Big Outside.

Scarlet gave tours sometimes and Cora's class had visited once with Signor Dragonfly. Cora had loved everything, from the overflowing crates, to the long wooden sorting counter, the tunnels and the different-sized chambers with their rows of neatly stacked shelves. The shelves were crammed with every item imaginable. There were aurochs horns – aurochs were a type of Stone Age cattle – feathers, fungi, flowers and leaves both dried and fresh, animal bones, teeth and a whole chamber dedicated to seeds. The stores were like a huge natural museum of the ages and Cora could have happily spent all day sorting through the amazing stuff there.

As the line shifted and Cora got closer to the front her heart grew wings and fluttered like a trapped butterfly against her ribs. Then it was Nis's turn. Scarlet's face lit up as Haru emptied his bag on the counter.

'Lovely work, Nis! Carrots and broccoli. Take them straight to the Crow's Nest. I'm sure your dad will find a use for them! Wild strawberries too – you have done well!'

Nis beamed with delight and Cora tapped her thumbs together at him in praise.

Trix was next. 'Self-heal, feathers, petals, a clump of fox fur and burdock burrs!' Scarlet's voice rose and she looked as if she might hug Trix. 'Burdock burrs are the bee's knees!'

'The bee's knees' was something Scarlet said when a Keeper had done something exceptionally good. Cora had high hopes of finding some bee's knees one day just to see what Scarlet said then.

'Look at the tiny hooks.' Scarlet handled the burdock with care to stop it attaching itself to her. 'This is perfect, just what I need for Grandmother Sky's car. Well done, Trix. I shall make sure that Grandmother Sky hears about this. I've been quite stuck recently and unable to move forward with my design, but the burdock burrs change everything. Come and see me in the workshop this afternoon. I'll show you how I'm going to use them.'

Trix almost floated out of the stores with delight. She loved building things, and Cora knew that an invitation to the workshop was her dream come true.

'Next,' said Haru, and the line moved forward again. Penelope got a well done for finding a pine cone. Winnie sent her a dark stare. Penelope ignored her and, fluffing up her long pink hair, she sent Cora a smug grin as she made for the door. Cora stuck her tongue out. Penelope's eyes narrowed furiously and Winnie sniggered.

It wasn't funny though. Cora was heavy with dread as Haru called Jax forward.

Chapter Five

Haru stared inside Jax's bag in confusion. 'A nut?' he said at last. 'A wrinkled nut and a bag of seeds that, if I'm not mistaken, were given to you before you went out. Is that it?'

'I expect it's a long story,' said Scarlet. She pointed to the end of the counter. 'Wait there,' she told Jax.

It was Cora's turn and for a second she wished she had been locked on the wrong side of the Bramble Door. She stepped forward and handed her bag to Haru, who carefully tipped it upside down. The bag of seeds fell out first, followed by, to her embarrassment, the garden fork, rake and spade because she hadn't secured them properly. The feather fluttered out last.

Scarlet's face darkened. 'That's it? And you were unable to finish planting the wildflower seeds, hmmm? Did you even start the task?'

Cora stared at her feet. Scarlet would be furious if she told her the truth about playing on the slide and losing track of time.

'Not good enough.' Scarlet's voice was dangerously low. 'I would send you back to school right now but I doubt that Signor Dragonfly would thank me for that! One more chance. Tomorrow you will do the task you are given and bring me a decent haul for the store or it'll be straight back to school for you both. Run along. Quickly, before I change my mind.' She flapped them away with her hands.

Cora was relieved they had been the last to return so there was no one else in the stores to see her shame.

'Want to go to the Crow's Nest to cheer ourselves up with acorn smoothies?' asked Jax, when they were outside.

'Maybe later.' Cora couldn't face anyone right now, and the cafe would be busy with Keepers hungry from working the morning shift.

Scarlet was not one for idle threats. If Cora and Jax didn't do the right thing tomorrow then she would have them back in school faster than an eye blink.

If only they hadn't messed about on the slide. They could have rewilded the land around the play park and there might even have been two eggshells to show Scarlet. It

could have earned them a *bee's knees* and a
mention to Grandmother Sky. Cora couldn't
shake the guilt nibbling at her. Keepers always
did their work and they didn't leave stuff
behind – especially precious stuff like eggshells.

Cora was still thinking about the play
park later that night when she snuggled
down under her leaf duvet. Nutmeg hopped
in through her open bedroom window,
scampered across the room and climbed on
her bed. Cora stroked the mouse's soft brown
fur. 'I'll go back there tomorrow,' she promised.

Cora gave Nutmeg a sunflower seed from
the twig pot on her bedside table. The twigs
were birch and Cora had tied them together
with plaited grass then decorated the pot
with painted stars when she was in nursery
class. 'I'll plant the wildflowers, and if there is
another eggshell there, I'll find it.'

★ ★ ★

Early the next morning Cora sat on the
bottom step outside her tree house sharing
her bark-bread toast with Nutmeg. The
little mouse's whiskers twitched as she
munched away. She was taking more than
her fair share of the toast but Cora didn't
mind. Her stomach was too knotty to eat.

She wished that
Jax would hurry
up and arrive so
they could get
on their way.
Cora wanted
to be at the
Bramble Door
the moment
it opened. She
couldn't wait to

show Scarlet that she was a good Keeper and
that she and Jax could work hard together.

Jax arrived silently, leaping out from behind a tree trunk. 'Boo!'

Cora jumped and dropped the bark bread. Nutmeg snatched it up and ran off, diving down between the twisty tree roots where she'd made her home.

'Whoops!' said Jax. 'I made you drop your bark-bread toast.'

'I didn't want it anyway.' Cora shouldered her woodland bag. 'We've got to do a proper job today. No messing around.'

'We will!' said Jax. 'We'll do our work and come back with our woodland bags bursting with good stuff.'

Cora wished she felt as confident, but often things didn't turn out the way she meant them to.

They were the first to arrive at the Bramble Door. Scarlet noticed their promising start.

'Hmm,' she said, but in a good way. 'Since you're here nice and early, you can have two jobs.' She handed them a bag of seeds each. 'You can go back to the play park and sow the wildflower seeds. Then you can go to the primary school and fix their pond. The side has collapsed and the frogs no longer have a shallow ledge to help them climb out. The frogs laid a lot of spawn this year, and the tiny froglets might drown if they can't get out of the water to rest and breathe.

'Eggshells are still on my Want List, and pine cones. I also need something comfortable to use for the seats in Grandmother Sky's new car. Something soft or squishy perhaps,' said Scarlet thoughtfully. 'Remember to stay out of sight and don't get caught by the Ruffins!'

As Cora and Jax went through the Bramble Door, Cora whispered, 'Let's go to the play park first.'

 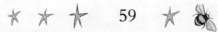

Jax sent her a sly look. 'For another go on the slide?'

'To do the job we were supposed to do yesterday,' said Cora indignantly. Is that what Jax thought of her? That having fun was more important than being a good Keeper? She hoped not!

A duck and her ducklings were out for an early morning swim in the river. Cora's heart melted when she saw the twelve fluffy babies paddling behind mum in a wonky line. Ordinarily, she would have stopped to watch them, but the threat of possibly being sent back to school weighed heavily in her mind. Nothing was going to distract her today. Not even cute little ducklings.

They walked over the river bridge and across the dew-soaked football field until they arrived at the play park. Cora and

Jax went around the outside, taking in the barren earth.

'We need to dig it over first,' said Jax.

They wriggled out of their woodland bags to get at their spades, rakes and bags of seed.

'Cattywumps!' said Jax, as he stuck his spade in the earth. 'It's as hard as nuts. This is going to take us ages.'

They dug carefully, gently lifting up earthworms and other creepy-crawlies and putting them to one side. Cora watched the sky anxiously as she worked. Would there be enough time to go to the school and search for another eggshell?

'Phew! That's it,' said Jax, standing back to admire the freshly turned soil. 'Let's give it a quick rake over.'

The raking didn't take long.

Cora grinned at Jax. 'Now for the fun part.' She dipped her hand into her bag of seeds and pulled out a fistful. 'Hi, lo, GROW!' she shouted, scattering them evenly over the soil.

'Sun shine, rain fall. Help our flowers sprout tall,' Jax added.

Cora and Jax spread out all of the wildflower seeds then carefully raked a thin layer of soil over the top to cover them up.

'Grow well, little seeds,' said Cora, crossing her finger over her thumb to wish them good luck. 'Before we go to the school, let's have a quick look round the play park. There might be another eggshell.'

Cora and Jax squeezed through the railings. They searched the play park but all they found was the pile of rubbish by the shelter. Cora's heart sank. There wasn't much spare time to tidy up, but she was determined to do the right thing today. She went to pick up a broken bottle, to put in the Ruffin bin, when

a sharp cry stopped her. Cora looked around. From under the bench in the shelter, two huge eyes watched her.

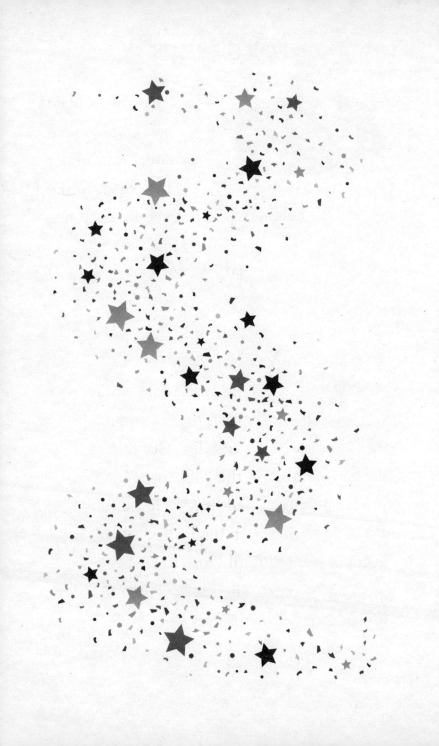

Chapter Six

It was a fox cub with an injured paw.

Cora gasped. 'You poor thing!'

The cub's paw was gashed and badly swollen. The fur around the wound was matted with blood and dirt. Cora thought the fox was one of the cubs that they'd seen yesterday. She walked slowly closer, carefully avoiding stepping on the broken glass. The little fox waited until Cora was within touching distance, then wriggled further under the bench. His eyes were wide and his breathing fast.

'I'm not going to hurt you.' Cora didn't want the cub to make the injury worse by struggling. Taking tiny steps towards him she whispered, 'Hold still, little fox. I'm going to help you.'

'What's happened?' asked Jax, coming up quietly beside her.

'He's cut his paw. I think he was looking for food in the pile of stuff I left behind yesterday. It's all my fault for not tidying up.'

'It's my fault too. And the Ruffins who made the mess.' Jax folded his arms. 'I ignored the rubbish. I was only interested in looking for a second eggshell.'

The cub began to whimper.

'I think I can help him.' Cora stretched out her hands. 'I'm going to use woodland magic to heal the wound,' she said. Cora focused on the cut and imagined it healing. Holding the picture in her mind she

❧ FOX CUB RESCUE ❧

wiggled her fingers and showered the cub's paw with a mist of sparkly magic. Fizzing and popping, the magic settled on the fox. Cora squinted at the wound hopefully. It had healed a little at the edges but that was all. Trying not to feel disheartened, she tried again.

'It's no good. My woodland magic isn't strong enough.'

The cub was growing more distressed. Yapping sharply, he wriggled away from Cora.

'Hush,' she soothed, daring to stroke his back. The cub stiffened and gave Cora a warning growl. 'I'm not going to hurt you,' she whispered, continuing to stroke him until he began to relax.

'Let's try combining our magic.' Jax stood close to Cora and put his hands over the wound just beside hers.

Cora imagined the skin growing back as she and Jax created a sparkly cloud of magic. The mist bubbled and hissed as it slowly evaporated. Eagerly Cora examined the fox's paw. Nothing had changed. The fox cub gave an impatient growl. He started to walk but squealed with pain, quickly raising his paw when he tried to put weight on it.

'What now?' said Jax. He looked around as if the answer might be hiding somewhere in the park.

Cora shut her eyes to think. There wasn't time to gather the plants needed to make a healing balm from scratch. 'Scarlet will have a ready-prepared healing balm in the stores,' she said slowly.

'Shall I run home and ask if we can have some?' Jax offered.

Cora fell quiet. Nice Cora wanted to help the fox cub. Not-so-nice Cora knew that if they asked Scarlet for a healing balm they would need to tell her what they wanted it for. That would lead to a much bigger explanation as to why they were in the play park and not at the school. Then Scarlet would definitely know that she and Jax had been messing around yesterday when they should have been working.

The fox cub broke into a high-pitched wail. Away in the distance Cora thought she heard the answering bark of an adult fox. The sound of it sent the little cub into a frenzy. Cora couldn't bear to see his distress. She was a bad Keeper. How could she even think about herself when the cub's injury was mostly her fault?

'Go!' she said to Jax. 'Tell Scarlet everything, and hurry.'

'We're going to help you.' Cora continued to stroke the cub. 'Jax, he's my friend, he's gone to get something to heal you. Jax is fast. I bet he could beat the wind if they raced.'

It wasn't long before Jax was back, tearing towards her across the field with Trix and Nis. Cora's heart sank. Trix and Nis were all very well, but where was the balm that Jax had gone for?

Jax pulled up by the fence and squeezed through the railings. Trix and Nis followed him. Jax clutched at his stomach as he caught his breath. 'Nis has gathered some more self-heal,' he gasped.

Trix took up the story. 'Nis and I had finished our rewilding task and were on our way home with the things we'd collected when we saw Jax. So, this is the cub?' Trix came closer. 'You're so cute. Don't be scared. We'll fix your paw in two shakes of your furry tail.'

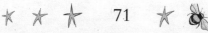

Nis pulled a handful of purple flowers with long green stems from his bag. Trix found two stones and used them to grind the plant to a sticky paste.

Nis and Trix were so organised, thought Cora as she watched Nis extract a handful of cobwebs and some tree leaves from his bag. It made her realise how much harder she needed to work if she wanted to be a good Keeper.

'Here's what we're going to do,' said Trix, taking charge. 'We're going to spread the paste on the fox's paw then bandage it with the cobweb and leaves. By the time the bandage falls off, the paw should be healed.'

Cora beamed. 'Did you hear that, little fox? You'll soon be walking again.'

Trix examined the cub's paw then carefully wove a bandage out of leaves. She grinned with satisfaction as she held it up. 'That should do it.'

Cora bit her lip as Nis went to apply the healing balm. Would he be able to do it without the fox struggling? The fox cub was watching her. 'We're not going to hurt you,' she said.

The fox seemed to trust her and stayed very still as Nis spread the gungy green paste over the cut. He finished by covering it with a layer of cobwebs.

'There, that wasn't too bad,' Cora told him. 'I'm not sure how he'll feel about the bandage though.' She cast a worried look at the fox cub as Trix began to wind the leaf bandage around his paw.

 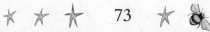

Suddenly the cub began to struggle.

'Gently!' Cora soothed.

Trix said through gritted teeth, 'I'm nearly done, but you need to keep him still.'

Speaking softly, Cora stroked the little fox's cheek. The cub's breath came warm and fast on her fingers and she hoped that he wouldn't bite her in fright. 'Hush,' she whispered. 'Stay still and soon you'll be able to run free.'

It seemed like ages before the cub started to relax, but eventually his breathing calmed and he stopped wriggling.

'Done,' said Trix, stepping back. She looked at her handiwork in pride. 'That should hold.'

Everyone stepped back to allow the fox to come out of the shelter. Cora held her breath. Had the balm worked? Would the fox cub be able to walk now?

The fox cub watched them warily. Cora waved her hand, gesturing for the others to move back under the swings. At last, the fox took a cautious step forward. Then another. He was limping quite badly. Cora noticed that he was trying to avoid putting weight on his injured paw. Would a sprinkling of woodland magic help now? It was worth a try. Cora stepped closer, and pointing her fingers at the fox's paw she showered it with a magical mist. The mist crackled and popped and when it cleared Cora saw that the swelling had gone.

'Off you go, back to your family.' Cora expected him to dash away but the fox hung back watching her warily. On timid paws he stepped forward and gratefully rubbed his head against her arm.

'I'm so sorry,' said Cora, rubbing him behind his ears.

A bark sounded behind her. Cora spun round and her heart leapt into her mouth. From the other side of the railings, the mother fox was watching her.

Chapter Seven

'Yap!' The fox cub bounced over to his mum, touching his nose to hers. She licked his face. The cub ran along the railings to a hole he must have dug to enter the park and, squeezing back through it, he joined his mum. Together, they ran towards Whispering Woods.

'Why did you tell the cub that you were sorry?' asked Trix curiously.

Cora flushed. 'Didn't Jax let on?' She shot him a grateful look. 'It was my fault that the cub got hurt. I didn't do a proper job yesterday. I saw the litter and left it here.'

'It was my fault too,' said Jax.

Very carefully, Cora began picking up the rubbish. There were several bottles and lots of wrappers.

Jax helped and they carried everything over to the Ruffin bin. As Cora put the last bottle into the bin, something caught her eye. On the ground, not far away, was a broken eggshell. It was the same creamy brown as the piece that Jax had found yesterday. *A wood pigeon*, thought Cora. The shell had broken

into two almost equal halves and was perfect
for filling with starlight-powered petals to
make car headlights. Cora should have felt
thrilled, but the experience with the fox cub
had left her feeling guilty and a little flat.
She handed the pieces of shell to Jax.

'No,' he said, shaking his head. 'One each.'

'Thanks.' Cora grinned back. Jax was a
good friend.

'Pooh!' Trix wrinkled her nose at the
stale odour coming from the rubbish bin.
'It smells like a Ruffin's big pongy feet. I
shouldn't worry about the fox. He looked
fine when he ran away.'

'I suppose.' Cora still felt bad.

'Time to go home,' said Nis. 'Dad's
baking honeysuckle doughnuts at the Crow's
Nest this morning. Honeysuckle doughnuts
sprinkled with crystallised dew drops and
acorn smoothies to drink, anyone?'

'Yum! I love your dad's doughnuts,' said Trix.

Cora shook her head. 'Can't. Jax and I haven't finished our rewilding yet. We've got to go to the primary school. You go on and we'll come by later.'

'The primary school?' Trix nodded at the sky. 'It's almost daylight. There's not enough time to get there and back *and* do your task.'

'We can't go back without doing it,' said Cora miserably. 'Look what happened to the fox cub. Some frogs urgently need our help. Anyway, if Scarlet finds out that we didn't finish our tasks, she'll send us back to school.'

'She wouldn't!' said Nis.

Cora and Jax exchanged a look – they both knew that Scarlet had said she would.

'What if a Ruffin sees you?' asked Trix.

Cora didn't need reminding of the danger. Sounding a lot braver than she felt, she said, 'We'll be quick and very careful.'

'I'm coming with you,' said Nis.

'Me too,' said Trix. 'We can get the job done in half the time if we help.'

'But . . .' said Cora.

'Wasting time,' said Trix. 'Let's go!'

Trix and Nis were the best, thought Cora. They knew the trouble they'd be in with Scarlet if they were late back. Worse still, what if the Bramble Door was locked? A thought suddenly exploded in Cora's brain. Trouble didn't really follow her around. She made things happen by her own choices. *From now on I'm going to work much harder,* she vowed.

The primary school was at the edge of the village. It had a huge playground and a playing field. The Keepers ran around looking for the pond.

'Ruffins aren't very logical,' said Cora as they covered all the grassy areas and didn't find any water. 'Where else would you put a pond?'

'Somewhere out of the way, so the Ruffin children don't fall in it?' Trix suggested.

'And close to the building so they don't have to walk too far to see it,' added Nis.

Cora wished they didn't have to get any closer to the school. What if there were Ruffins about already? But taking risks was all part of the job. The best Keepers didn't avoid danger.

The school was built in a square around a paved courtyard with a wooden gate. Near the gate was a flower garden with rocks in amongst the flowers. Cora, Jax, Nis and Trix rolled one of the rocks over to the gate and climbed on it to reach the latch. Once they were in the courtyard, Cora felt the ends of her hair fizzling as they tiptoed past a long row of windows. What if someone was working inside?

'Pooh,' said Jax, his nose wrinkling. 'Ruffin schools smell funny, even outside.'

'I think it's that sock,' said Nis, pointing at a soggy sock underneath a wooden bench.

Trix giggled. 'Somewhere, there's a very young Ruffin with one cold foot.'

'How?' said Cora, bewildered. 'How could you not notice that you'd lost a sock? Eew!' she added. She used a spritz of woodland magic to make the

sock hop on to the bench where the owner might find it.

'There's the pond.' Jax walked over to a circular patch of grass in the middle of the courtyard. The pond was sunk into the grass and had reeds growing around the edge. The water was muddy brown. Several froglets were resting on a lily pad in the middle of the water. Just as Scarlet had said, they seemed to be stranded as there wasn't a ledge at the side of the pond to help them climb out.

'How are we going to fix this?' asked Cora.

Trix had one of her brilliant ideas. 'Let's roll that boulder we used at the gate over here. We can put it in the water to make a stepping stone. If we cover it with mud and pondweed, the Ruffins won't know it's there and remove it again.'

It took a while to push the heavy boulder over to the pond.

'Gently,' warned Trix, as they prepared to lower it into the water. 'We don't want to squash any of the wildlife.'

Like a huge, stompy Ruffin's foot squashing us, Cora thought with a shudder. Carefully they pushed the boulder into the water and

camouflaged it with mud and weeds from
the edge of the pond.

'Perfect!' said Trix. 'It's exactly the right
size for a ledge, and you'd never guess it was
a stone taken from the garden.'

The pond rippled and two eyes broke
the surface. Trix squeaked and jumped back,
almost knocking Cora over.

'It's a frog!' Cora was delighted. The frog
clambered on to the stone ledge and out of
the pond. Its mouth opened and closed as it
watched the Keepers warily.

'It worked!'
said Jax happily.
In the distance
the Horn of Tyr
sounded.
'Good timing
too,' said Cora.
'We have to go.'

'Wait. There is something else!' Trix sprinted across the courtyard to a shady corner. 'Look at this wall. It's covered with moss.'

'Yes, very pretty,' said Cora. She ran over with Jax and Nis. 'We have to go.'

'But don't you see?' Trix's eyes were shining. 'Scarlet wanted something soft to make car seats for Grandmother Sky's car. This is perfect, and there's enough for us to take some.'

She waved her hand at the wall, sprinkling it with woodland magic. There was a hiss and then a portion of the moss peeled away and slid to the ground. Trix rolled it up and held it out to Cora. 'Scarlet's going to be thrilled.'

'She is too!' Cora badly wanted to be the one who gave the moss to Scarlet, but Trix had found it. Lovely, clever Trix who was still waving the rolled-up moss at Cora and insisting that she took it. It was tempting. She bet that Trix already had a lot of stuff in her woodland bag . . .

Trix was looking dreamy. Cora knew that expression – it was Trix's inventing look. Right now, Trix would be working out all the different ways the moss could be used to make Grandmother Sky's car seats soft and bouncy. Whereas all Cora could think of was how the moss would make a brilliant trampoline for her and Jax. For a tiny peck, Cora was tempted to take the moss from Trix, but she knew that wasn't fair. Trix deserved the moss more than her. If she took it to Scarlet, she would definitely get a *bee's knees* and maybe another *come and see me in the workshop*. Trix would also get her name written in Grandmother Sky's party book.

'Just take it,' said Nis.

'Trix found it!' Jax backed Cora up.

'Take it. I don't want Scarlet to send you back to school!' Trix shook the moss at Cora.

'She won't. We've got the eggshells, remember!'

Trix threw the moss to Cora.

Cora caught it and went to throw it back, but Trix put her hands behind her back. Cora smiled and gave in. 'Thanks, Trix. I owe you loads.'

'Forget it. It's time to go home.'

Cora wriggled out of her woodland bag and stored the moss inside. Now she had the moss and the eggshell, but after yesterday's oak-tree-sized fail, would it be enough to please Scarlet?

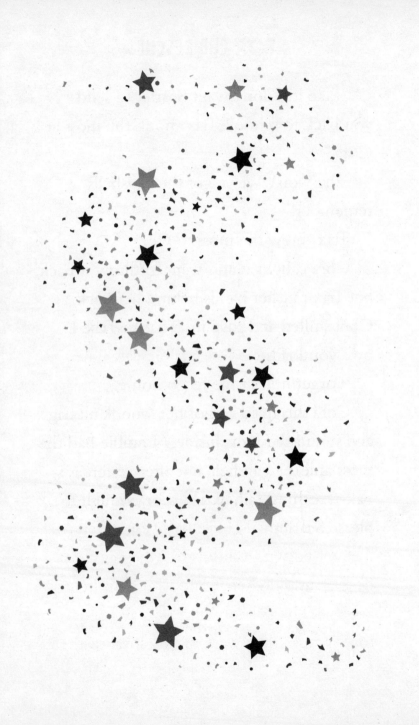

Chapter Eight

The four friends hurried across the football field towards the cafe. The same Ruffin from yesterday was opening it up, only this time he wasn't alone. A black dog with a smooth shiny coat ambled along at his side.

Something fluttered in Cora's chest. She loved animals, but dogs were different. They lived with Ruffins and they could be dangerous. The fierce ones you definitely avoided. The friendly ones you avoided too, because they were mostly loyal to their

Ruffin. They also had slobbery tongues, hairy bottoms and tails that could flatten a Keeper with one cheerful wag.

'Dog ahead!' Cora warned.

'Seen it!'

The Ruffin and his dog were walking a different way. Jax, who was in the lead, changed course, widening the distance between them. Cora wished the football field wasn't so open. There was nowhere to hide, and the Whispering Woods on the other side of the river seemed a lifetime away. Silently she ran on with one eye on the dog.

With no warning, it suddenly whipped up its head and sniffed the air. In a flash it sprinted away from its Ruffin. Cora felt sick. The dog had caught their scent, but was it coming to say hello or to catch them?

'Hide!' yelled Jax. He pointed to a thick clump of nettles growing in front of the river bridge.

The nettle patch wasn't that big but it was the only cover there was. Cora ran faster. They'd got this! Nettles didn't bother Keepers, but she'd heard that they stung like wasps if you were a Ruffin or a dog.

Jax reached the nettles and slid between them. Trix and Nis arrived together, piling into the nettles and disappearing. The dog was gaining on Cora. Hands appeared from between the nettle stems as Jax, Trix and Nis reached out to help her. She was so close but then a blast of hot breath hit her from behind, almost blowing her over. She heard the thud of paws and panting breath. Time for woodland magic.

Cora pointed at her toes, but in her panic she missed and blasted the grass. It erupted at once, squeaking and creaking as the blades shot upwards. *Could have been worse,* Cora decided as she dodged between the growing blades. At least the grass gave her some cover. She pointed at her toes again and this time scored. On superfast feet she reached the nettle bed and dived inside.

Cora's heart thundered and she was struggling to catch her breath when the nettles exploded apart. Cora jumped backwards as a black nose with twitchy nostrils rushed towards her.

'Over here!' Jax called, but the dog cut Cora off before she could move. Trix's and Nis's shouts for the dog to *leave* were almost drowned out as the dog crashed closer to Cora. It was hard to stay calm, but Cora aimed her magic at the dog, hoping to make him lie down. A puff of mist spluttered from her fingers then evaporated. Cora tried again but it was too soon after using her magic to run faster. She grabbed a nettle stem and, snapping it from the plant, she used it like a sword, jabbing it at the dog. It wasn't much of a weapon, but a sting on the nose might slow the dog enough for her to escape.

The dog thought it was a game. Barking, he jumped up and down, trying to snatch the nettle from Cora.

'Leave!' She ran backwards, waving her nettle frantically.

The dog pounced without warning. Mouth open, he snatched Cora up by her woven grass top. Cora caught a flash of sharp fangs, then she swung round. Staring at the sky she dangled helplessly from the dog's jaws.

'Put me down!' she yelled, thrusting her nettle at the dog's nose. It was harder than trying to catch fireflies – Cora kept missing as she swung this way and that. The dog was playing with her, shaking her from side to side until she could hardly breathe. Then suddenly she was falling.

Cora hit the ground with a *whumph*, the air rushing from her lungs. There was more shouting and a mist of magic swirled round the dog. Cora was aware of Jax, Trix and Nis pointing at him. The dog's head was nodding and his eyes began to close. Were they trying to make him fall asleep?

Cora scrambled up. The dog snapped to attention again and wobbled towards her. Cora froze, not daring to move as she stared up at him.

'Hector!' called a Ruffin voice. 'Hector, come here.'

The dog eyeballed Cora. She eyeballed him back even though she was shaking inside. Footsteps approached at a run.

'Hector. Here, boy.' A shadow fell over the nettle patch. Cora could hardly breathe as the Ruffin reached for his pocket. For a net? It was how they captured Keepers, wasn't it? But the Ruffin pulled out a bone-shaped biscuit and snapped it in half. As the biscuit cracked, Hector spun round, spraying Cora with drool. Cora's breath whooshed out. Thank goodness Hector liked biscuits more than he liked Keepers.

'Good boy.' There was the crunch of teeth on biscuit and the snap of a lead being clipped to a collar. The nettles shook as the Ruffin left with Hector obediently trotting by his side.

Cora almost collapsed in a heap, but five sharp blasts on Tyr stopped her. The final warning.

'No!' she gasped. They couldn't be late home again.

Chapter Nine

C ora, Jax, Trix and Nis ran through the woods, leaping over small roots, weaving round large ones. Jax in the lead, his blue hair trailing behind him like a banner, kept yelling encouragement back at the others. Cora was conscious of her woodland bag bumping up and down on her back. What would be scarier – getting locked out or breaking the eggshell? If this shell got damaged then she and Jax would be sent back to school for sure.

Then suddenly she saw a straggle of
Keepers ahead. Relief flooded through Cora.
They weren't as late as yesterday.

'We've got this!' she shouted.

Summoning every last bit of energy, Cora
ran on, arriving at the Bramble Door with
very little breath left.

'Take your bags to the stores,' said Scarlet.
She checked her poppy-seed-powered
watch. Two Keepers slipped inside behind

Cora. Scarlet pulled
out a key-shaped twig,
then shutting the
door, she locked it.
Cora could feel
Scarlet's eyes boring
into her woodland
bag as she followed
them through the
trees to the stores.

'Have we done enough?' she hissed
to Jax as they queued to have their bags
checked.

'I think so,' he replied.

Scarlet was very pleased with Trix and
Nis. 'Feathers, herbs, wild garlic, more self-
heal and two pine cones. You've come back
with so much useful stuff. Keep this up and
it won't be long before I can sign you off as
trainees and make you fully trained Keepers,'
she said. 'Well done, you two. Go and have a
well-earned break.'

Trix and Nis exchanged a grin with Cora
and Jax as they left.

It was Jax's turn. Cora waited in agony
as he stepped forward, but she needn't have
worried. Scarlet was delighted with the
eggshell.

'Well!' said Scarlet holding it up. 'A wood
pigeon's eggshell. Very good work, Jax. What

 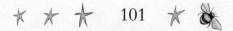

a shame you broke the other one. But still, this is excellent work.' She smiled kindly at him. 'And you completed two tasks today. I knew you had it in you. Away you go then.'

Jax didn't need to be told twice. He skipped out of the stores before Scarlet changed her mind, crossing his finger over his thumb and holding them up to Cora to wish her luck as he passed.

Cora had a forest full of fireflies flittering in her tummy as Haru emptied her bag and stood back for Scarlet to inspect the contents.

'Hmmm,' said Scarlet. 'Hmmm,' she added, her voice rising when she saw the eggshell. She stared at it in disbelief. 'Am I seeing things? Is this really a matching pair?' She put it next to the piece that Jax had brought in. 'Remarkable! They're clearly from the same egg. Better still, they're perfect. Once

they're filled
with petals along
with a hearty
dash of starlight,
Grandmother

Sky's new car will have the brightest
headlights a Keeper could ever want. *From
nature's floor to our door, caring for the countryside
and taking only what we need!* It's what we
Keepers do best.' Scarlet looked so thrilled
that for a worrying second Cora thought she
was going to jump over the counter and hug
her!

Then someone behind Cora in the
queue cheered and everyone yodelled and
clapped. Scarlet shook her head, but she
was smiling as she carefully handed the
eggshells to Haru to put somewhere safe.
Turning back to Cora she said, 'Excellent
work.'

 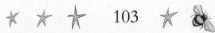

Cora flushed with pleasure as Scarlet picked up the roll of moss and inhaled sharply.

'Moss! Feel how soft this is.' She held it out to Haru. 'This is incredible work, Cora. Grandmother Sky will be most impressed when she hears about you.' Scarlet drew another breath in. 'You completed two tasks today and you brought me two of the things on my Want List. Grandmother Sky will probably write your name in her book.'

'Wait!' Cora couldn't bear it a moment longer. It was bad enough to let Scarlet think that she'd found the moss. But to dupe Grandmother Sky *and* to have her name written in the book so that it counted towards an invitation to a palace party ... It wouldn't be fair to Trix, who deserved it much more than she did. Cora hated unfairness, even though telling the truth was likely to get her into big trouble.

'Trix found the moss, not me,' she confessed, and the whole story came tumbling out. The play park, the big slide, running out of time and how it had led to the first eggshell getting smashed. Returning to the play park the following day and finding the cub. Cora left nothing out.

'Well!' said Scarlet, her lips thinning as Cora gasped out her last sentence.

Cattywumps! She wasn't good enough to be a trainee. Scarlet would definitely send her back to school.

'Well!' Something strange was happening. Scarlet's lips were twitching as if she was trying not to smile. 'I should be very cross with you both. Yes, you too, Jax. Don't think that I can't see you hiding outside the door.'

Jax sidled back into the storeroom and came over to stand by Cora.

'Being a Keeper isn't easy, but it's what we do and we do it with pride. Work always comes first when we are in the Big Outside. But I think you both know that. In fact, I know that you do, or you wouldn't have tried to put right your mistakes. There is no need for me to punish you . . . but I shall be keeping an eye on you both. If you want to become fully trained Keepers and not be sent back to school, then please try to stay out of trouble in future.'

'We will. Thank you, Scarlet.' Cora and Jax hurried outside.

'Celebratory spin,' said Cora in relief. She crossed her arms and held her hands out to Jax. Crossing his, he grabbed hold of Cora and they spun each other round in a circle until they fell down, giddy.

'We can do this, Jax. It won't be long before we're proper Keepers!'

'Keepers,' Jax repeated with a soppy grin.

'Let's go and find Trix and Nis. I bet they're at the Crow's Nest scoffing honeysuckle doughnuts with sprinkles.'

'Honeysuckle doughnuts, yum! Race you there,' said Jax, immediately sprinting away.

 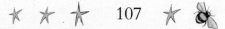

'Cheat,' said Cora. But she was too happy to mind much. 'I can't wait for our next outing,' she shouted after him. 'I love being a Keeper and caring for the countryside.'

The End

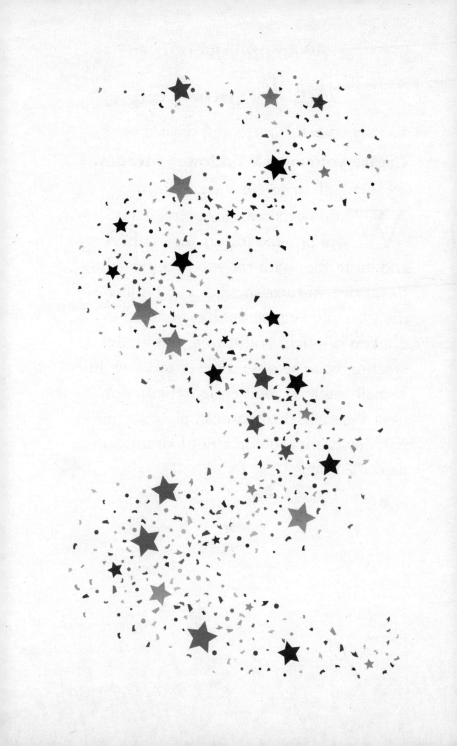

The Keeper Way

Create your own Wildflower Meadow

Wildflowers are very pretty. They also provide insects such as bees and butterflies with the food they need to survive. In turn, these insects pollinate the fruit and vegetables that we need to eat. You can help pollinators, and us, by creating your own wildflower meadow in a small patch of your garden. If you don't have a garden, then you can plant a mini wildflower meadow in a pot like the one described here.

Things you will need

* A flower pot or other container such as a clean ice-cream tub

* Peat-free compost or soil

* Wildflower seeds – you can buy a mixed packet or mix your own seeds together such as cornflowers, wild poppies, corn marigolds, corn buttercups and ragged robin.

Planting your Wildflower Meadow

Check that your pot has drainage holes in the bottom. If you need to make some holes then ask an adult to help you.

Fill your pot with the compost or soil up to approximately 2 cm from the top.

Scatter the wildflower seeds on top.

Lightly cover with a layer of compost or soil.

Leave on a windowsill, balcony or other outside space.

Water regularly and wait for your flowers to grow.

Acknowledgements

It takes a team and a brilliant illustrator to bring a book to life. I could not have asked for lovelier people to work with me on Woodland Magic. To name a few:

Polly Nolan, who is wonderful and just the best agent.

Maurice Lyon – it's always a joy to work with you.

Everyone at Piccadilly Press for your enthusiasm and support.

Katy Riddell – thank you for bringing Woodland Magic to life with your amazing illustrations. You've captured Cora and her world exactly how I imagined it.

My ever-patient family and friends, especially Will and Tim, who are luckily now grown-up enough to cook when I forget, and Antonia, who cooks *and* argues over commas!

Dad and my late Mum, who bought every book I wrote in vast quantities to give to everyone.

And Alistair – LYFB.

Julie Sykes

As a child, Julie was always telling tales.
Not the 'she ate all the cake, not me' kind,
but wildly exaggerated tales of everyday
events. Julie still loves telling stories and
is now the bestselling author of more
than 100 books for children of all ages
and is published around the world. She
has recently moved to Cornwall with
her family and a white wolf – cunningly
disguised as a dog. When she's not writing
she likes eating cake, reading and walking,
often at the same time.

Katy Riddell

Katy grew up in Brighton and was obsessed with drawing from a young age, spending many hours writing and illustrating her own stories, which her father (award-winning illustrator Chris Riddell) collected. Katy rediscovered her love for illustrating children's books after graduating with a BA Hons in Illustration and Animation from Manchester Metropolitan University. She loves working with children and lives and works in Brighton.

Protecting nature is magic for the secret little Keepers

Look out for more adventures from the Nature Keepers.

Read on for an extract from
Woodland Magic: Deer in Danger . . .

Cora could hardly bear to look. She covered her face with her hands, watching between her fingers. At the very last moment, the deer noticed the fence and jumped. Cora saw hooves and rusty brown fur. A few seconds later she heard the clatter of Ruffin metal and a loud crash. A panicked screech pierced her ears, and then it went silent.

Cora and Jax ran over. The flimsy metal fence, held up with the concrete blocks, had broken and a large section lay on the ground. The fence was made up of smaller metal squares. Carefully, they jumped across it.

'Where did the deer go?' asked Jax.

'Over here.' Cora reached a piece of pegged string and ducked under it. Weirdly, she now found herself level with the deer's head. She looked again. The rest of the deer was trapped in a deep trench. His nostrils flared and he trotted forward until he reached the end of the trench, but there was no way out. The sides were too steep to climb and there wasn't any room for him to jump.

'Stay still!' Cora couldn't bear to see the deer's distress as he scrabbed to be free.

Jax came up beside her. 'Is he hurt?'

Cora shook her head. 'I don't think so, but he's terrified.'

'I'm going to help him. Hold onto me.' Cora waited for Jax to put his arms around her waist then leaned into the trench. She stroked the deer's rusty brown shoulder. 'Hello you,' she said softly.

The deer stared up at Cora with huge, frightened eyes. He arched his back and kicked out, trying to break free.

'Stay still. You're going to hurt yourself.' Cora stretched out her fingers and sprinkled the deer with Woodland Magic. It crackled as it fell in sparkles on the deer's back. Cora imagined him floating out of the trench.

The deer snorted in surprise as he rose up a pip.

Cora held her breath – was her Woodland magic strong enough?

It wasn't. An eye-blink later the deer's hooves hit the ground with a soft thud.

Cora frowned, dragging her hands through her hair as she tried to recall some of the more useful things she'd learned at school. 'Remember that lesson with Signor Dragonfly when we made that pulley and a sling to lift each other over the brook?'

Jax chuckled. 'We were racing with Trix and Nis, only we crashed into Perfect Penelope. Everyone fell in the water and Penelope got tangled in starwort.'

'Not that bit,' said Cora, grinning at the memory of Penelope with mud dripping down her face, her perfect pink hair turned green from the starwort. 'The bit when we made the pulley. What did we use?'

Jax scratched his head. 'A grass blanket, sticks, woven vines and a small wheel, I think.'

'Could we make something similar to winch the deer out?'

'It might work,' said Jax. 'But what would we use?'

Cora and Jax searched the immediate area, looking for things both natural or Ruffin-made that the Ruffins had left behind. Cora found a thick plastic bag caught beneath the wheel of a cement mixer. The bag was empty except for a few particles of sand stuck to the inside. Nervously she approached the machine, not trusting it to stay still even though Signor Dragonfly had taught them that Ruffin machines needed a special key to make them work.

The bag felt nasty. Cora gritted her teeth as she pulled on the plastic. At first it didn't budge, so Jax came over to help her. With the extra pair of hands, the top of the bag thinned and stretched, leaving the rest of it firmly trapped beneath the giant wheel.

'Stuck fast,' Jax panted. 'We'll have to find something else.' He stood back with his hands on his hips and stared up at the machine. 'If only we had a Ruffin key. We could use the dumper truck to lift the deer out with the scoop.'

'Too dangerous!' said Cora firmly. She was suddenly anxious that he might climb up the machine and find its key. 'The machine's so big. We could hurt the deer if we got it wrong.'

Then she thought of a plan. She glanced around her. The sky was grey and silent. She couldn't hear any birds bringing in the dawn with their noisy chorus. If she was quick, there was enough time to put it into action.

'I'm going home,' she announced. 'I'll ask Scarlet to lend me something from the stores to make a pulley and sling so we can lift the deer up out of the trench.'

'Want me to wait with the deer or come with you?' Jax asked.

'Come with me.' Cora smiled at him gratefully. Jax was a brilliant friend. They both knew it would be far too dangerous for him to wait on the Ruffin building site alone.